NEW HAVEN FREE PUBLI

W9-DAE-885

3 5000 07177 3468

DATE DUE

OCT 18 1999		
MAY 2 2000		
MAR 17 2001		
APR 2 1 2003		
OCT 27 2003		
MAY 17 2007 — ILL		
JUL 13 2009		
JUL 8 2013		
FEB 2 5 2015		

JENNY'S
ADOPTED
BROTHERS

Written and Illustrated by
Esther Averill

GLOUCESTER, MASS.

PETER SMITH

1987

OTHER JENNY
BOOKS ARE:

The Cat Club
The School for Cats
Jenny's First Party
Jenny's Moonlight
Adventure
When Jenny Lost
Her Scarf

JENNY'S ADOPTED BROTHERS
Copyright, 1952, by Esther Averill
Printed in the United States of America
All rights in this book are reserved

Library of Congress catalog card number: 52-7849

Reprinted, 1987, by arrangement with
Harper & Row, Publishers

ISBN 0-8446-6286-0

THE little black cat, Jenny Linsky, sat down beside the rosebush in her master's garden. The roses were in bloom, the birds were singing and the sun shone brightly.

"How lucky I am to have this garden and a master like the Captain," thought Jenny. "I wish every cat could have the nice things I have."

3

At that moment Jenny was surprised to see a black and white cat sitting alone in a corner of the garden.

"There's a cat I've never seen before," continued Jenny. "He looks as if he wanted something. He's bigger than I, but maybe I can help him."

Jenny straightened the red scarf she was wearing, and ran over to the stranger.

"Hello," she said. "My name is Jenny Linsky. What's yours?"

The stranger removed a red ball he was holding in his mouth, and said, "My name is Checkers."

"Checkers what?" asked Jenny.

"I can't remember my last name," said Checkers. "So much has happened that I've forgotten lots of things."

"Checkers is a very pretty name," said Jenny in a comforting voice. "And it's a good name for you," she added as she examined the furry, black checks on his thin, white legs. "But you look hungry. Don't they feed you at home?"

"I haven't any home," said Checkers.

"No home?" cried Jenny. "Oh, it isn't fair! Why, Checkers, I have this lovely garden and that brick house with the ivy on it. And my master, Captain Tinker, is the nicest master in the world."

As she gazed at Checkers' darling, heart-shaped face, she had a bright idea.

"Checkers," she said, "I'm Captain Tinker's only cat. If you'll come home with me, I'll ask the Captain to adopt you."

"Thank you," cried Checkers joyfully. "I'll go with you as soon as Edward comes."

"Edward? Who is he?" asked Jenny.

"Edward is my big brother," replied Checkers. "His last name is Brandywine. We met when both of us lost our homes, and we've been brothers ever since. Where I go, Edward goes too."

"Checkers," sighed Jenny, "maybe my master isn't rich enough to adopt two—"

Jenny didn't have time to finish her sentence. Edward had heard his name, and he came hurrying out of the bushes.

He was a tiger cat with a broad, white chest and beautiful eyes. But in those eyes there was the sad look of cats who have no homes.

"Edward," said Checkers, "this is Jenny Linsky. She's going to ask her master, Captain Tinker, to adopt us."

Just then a bell rang in the garden.

"That's the Captain calling me to lunch," explained Jenny.

Checkers picked up his red ball and started toward the Captain's house.

But Jenny said, "Wait. It isn't easy to get *two* cats adopted. We must work out a plan."

She thought hard for a moment and then

8

said, "I have it. I'll try to get you adopted one at a time."

"Jenny," begged Edward, "please try to get Checkers adopted first. He's smaller than I, and very hungry. I'll wait outside your house until you call me. If you don't call me, I'll know the Captain hasn't enough room for me."

"Edward!" cried Checkers. "Didn't you and I promise to stick together?"

Edward gazed up toward the point where the tall buildings of the city scraped the sky. His right nostril twitched. "I smell a storm," he murmured. "By night we shall have rain."

Then he looked tenderly at Checkers and said, "Another night outdoors in the cold rain might make you sick. Please go with Jenny into Captain Tinker's house. Show him the retrieving trick I taught you. I'm sure he'll adopt you when he sees how nicely you retrieve."

"Retrieve? What's that?" asked Jenny.

"To retrieve means to run after something and bring it back," explained Checkers. "This red ball I carry everywhere is my retrieving ball."

At that moment the lunch bell sounded for the second time.

"We mustn't keep the Captain waiting," said Jenny. "Checkers, when we get home, you must retrieve for us."

The three cats ran toward Captain Tinker's house. On the way Jenny asked Edward, "Can you retrieve too?"

"No," he answered. "There's no trick I can do. But some day, if I find a home that has a little office in it, I should like to write."

"Write what?" asked Jenny.

"Write about the troubles I've had," replied Edward.

When the cats reached the house, Edward crawled into the bushes near the open win-

dow, and Jenny led Checkers through the window, into the living room.

Captain Tinker who was an old sailor, was sitting in his armchair, waiting for Jenny.

He must have been surprised to see her bringing home a black and white cat, with a heart-shaped face, who held a red ball in his mouth.

But the Captain was polite to cats. He let Jenny speak first.

She whispered to Checkers, "Retrieve."

Checkers passed his ball to Jenny. "Hit it hard," he said.

She batted it across the floor. He bounded after it, caught it with his teeth, returned with it and laid it at the Captain's feet.

The Captain said to Checkers, "That was the most beautiful retrieving I've ever seen. And such a pretty ball!"

Checkers whispered to Jenny, "Hit the ball again. I must retrieve some more to help get Edward adopted."

But Captain Tinker picked up the ball, and looking thoughtfully at Checkers, said, "You're hungry, and a red ball never filled an empty stomach. You must stay and eat some lunch with Jenny. After that—why, after that, you may live with us forever, if you wish."

"Checkers," cried Jenny happily, "you've been adopted. Now I'll call Edward."

She turned toward the window. To her surprise she saw that Edward had come to the window sill without waiting to be called.

On his striped face there was a look that Jenny had never seen on any cat. It was the look of a cat gazing at something warm and beautiful which he may have to leave because he is not wanted.

"Oh!" thought Jenny. "The Captain mustn't send Edward away; it would break his heart. I must speak to the Captain about this and try to make him understand."

Jenny was on the point of jumping onto her master's knees to plead for Edward, when the Captain caught sight of the face at the window. And he saw Checkers glance quickly at the face. Then Checkers sat very straight and still, like someone wishing hard for something to come true.

"These two cats belong together," murmured Captain Tinker.

Without another word he walked to the window and pulled Edward gently into the room. In that way Edward was adopted.

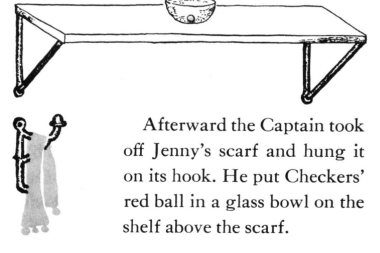

Afterward the Captain took off Jenny's scarf and hung it on its hook. He put Checkers' red ball in a glass bowl on the shelf above the scarf.

Then the Captain said to Edward, "You haven't a red ball and you haven't a red scarf. But you shall soon have something red, so that everyone will know you are one of us. After lunch I'll make you a red leather collar."

"My!" thought Jenny. "How quickly things have happened. My brothers came. They were adopted. What will happen next?"

Jenny and her brothers followed Captain Tinker into the kitchen. There he put two extra plates on Jenny's feeding tray, and filled all three of the plates with carrots and beef.

The brothers could not believe their eyes. It was so long since they had seen a meal like this. They tried to purr their thanks to Captain Tinker. But their purrs got mixed with their food.

Each mouthful that the brothers ate put new life into their tired bodies. When lunch was over and they had washed their faces, Checkers and Edward looked like happy cats. Jenny no longer felt sorry for them.

Edward turned to her and asked politely, "Do you think the Captain has a little office where I might do some writing?"

"Captain Tinker has gone down to his workshop in the cellar," replied Jenny. "I'll take you through our house. I'm sure you'll find an office somewhere."

Jenny led Edward and Checkers up the stairs. At the top of the stairs she said proudly, "Our house has three floors. This is the second floor, and—"

Suddenly Jenny remembered the day when she herself was adopted by Captain Tinker. The Captain, after rescuing her from trouble in the street, had brought her into this same house and allowed her to explore it by herself, the way cats like to do.

So Jenny told her brothers, "You may explore this second floor. I'll wait for you downstairs."

Jenny returned to the living room and waited on the sofa. While she waited, she could hear the brothers exploring overhead, from room to room. With each step and sniff they made, she felt that Checkers and Edward were becoming more and more a part of this dear home where she had always been the only cat.

Soon Checkers came pattering down the stairs.

"Edward has found an office," he announced to Jenny. "It's in a closet, behind the Captain's rubber boots."

Behind the Captain's rubber boots!

Jenny gulped. . . . That was a place where she liked to doze on rainy days. And it was raining now.

The storm which Edward predicted had burst on the garden.

"How dark the garden looks!" exclaimed Checkers. "It's as black as night. I guess I'll take a nap."

Without asking Jenny's permission, he climbed into the Captain's armchair and fell asleep.

Jenny wished that Checkers had chosen another place for his nap.

"I know he's tired," she thought crossly. "But I'm the only cat who has ever slept in Captain Tinker's armchair."

Then she wondered what Edward was doing: "I bet he isn't writing at all. I bet he's snoozing."

Jenny tiptoed up the stairs. As she passed Edward's office in the closet, she could hear the sound of heavy breathing mingled with delicate snores.

"Just what I thought," she told herself. "Well, if everyone else can take a nap, I have a right to take one too. Maybe I'll feel better after it."

Jenny went into the Captain's bedroom, crawled into her basket and fell sound asleep. When she awakened at supper time, she felt rested and cheerful.

"From now on I'll share everything with Checkers and Edward," she decided as she went down the stairs.

But when she entered the living room, her heart turned cold with jealousy.

Captain Tinker was sitting in his armchair. On one of his knees sat Checkers. On the other knee sat Edward wearing a new, red leather collar!

Jenny rushed toward her brothers.

"The Captain's knees belong to me," she cried. "Get down!"

Checkers and Edward jumped quickly to the floor.

Then the Captain picked up Jenny, stroked her cheek and said, "Jenny, don't be jealous of your brothers. I love you just as much as ever."

But Jenny was too upset to believe him. Before she knew what she was doing she had scratched the Captain's hand. Then, frightened by her awful deed, she fled to a safe place beneath the sofa.

Captain Tinker did not call after her or scold her. Instead, he walked quietly into the kitchen and washed the scratch. Next, he opened the door of the icebox. Jenny could hear him take out the supper food, warm it and fill the three plates on her tray. After that, he returned to his workshop in the cellar.

"I know why the Captain has left me," thought Jenny. "He wants me to make friends with my brothers. But I won't do it. Maybe I shall never speak to them again. Anyway, I'll let them eat their supper by themselves."

She listened, but could not hear Checkers and Edward go into the kitchen. She could not hear them in the living room. Fear gripped her heart. Perhaps she'd been so horrid that her brothers had run off to find another home.

Jenny rushed into the kitchen. The brothers were not there, and they had not touched their supper.

She rushed upstairs and could not find them anywhere.

She ran downstairs and jumped onto the shelf.

Checkers' red retrieving ball was gone!

"That's it," she moaned. "He's taken his ball and run off with Edward. And on a night like this! Why, they may die of cold and hunger. I'll go after them, and I won't come home until I've found them."

Jenny dashed out into the rain. She splashed across the garden, climbed over the fence and ran down the alley into South Street. There she could not tell which way to turn. The rain had washed away all traces of her brothers' paws.

She decided to turn to the right, and ran through swirling puddles, while the rain drenched her back and filled her ears. On and on she ran, looking in every doorway. But she could not find her brothers.

At last she felt that she was running the wrong way. She stopped and asked herself, "Where would I go on a rainy night, if I were homeless? I'd go to the fish shop, and wait in the doorway, and hope that in the morning someone would give me some fish for breakfast."

Jenny turned back on her trail, and worked her way through the soaking rain until she reached the fish shop. There, huddled in the doorway, sat her brothers.

"Checkers! Edward!" she cried. "I've been mean and selfish. Please forgive me and come home."

26

"Jenny," said Edward gravely, "Checkers and I must try to find another home. We don't feel you want us in your house."

"I do want you," she protested.

"Do you love us?" asked Checkers.

"With all my heart," she cried. "To prove how much I love you, I'll let you and Edward sleep every night in my own basket in the Captain's bedroom. I'll sleep in the cellar."

"Jenny, that proves you really love us," declared Edward. "We'll go home with you. But we won't take your basket. *We'll* sleep in the cellar."

"No, I'll sleep in the cellar," Jenny said.

"No, we will," said the brothers.

"I will," insisted Jenny. Then she added quickly, "Let's not argue now, for we should hurry home. I want to find the Captain and beg him to forgive me for scratching his hand."

Jenny and her brothers ran home through the rain. When they reached the house they found the Captain waiting anxiously for them, with bath towels to rub them dry.

As he rubbed Jenny's fur she tucked her chin in the hand she had scratched, and begged him to forgive her.

"Oh, that was just a little scratch," said Captain Tinker. "You made up for it when you ran out into the rainy night to find your brothers."

Then Jenny tried to tell the Captain about the sleeping basket. But he said briskly, "Go now and eat your supper."

So she went into the kitchen with Checkers and Edward, and ate supper.

After that, the Captain said to her, "It's very late, and time for all good cats to be in bed. Come, see what I have built for your two brothers."

Jenny and her brothers followed Captain Tinker up the stairs. In the room next to his bedroom stood two little bunks that he had built one above the other. Each bunk had a warm red blanket on it.

"Now no one will have to sleep in the cellar," cried Jenny happily, while her brothers rubbed their backs against the Captain's legs and thanked him.

Checkers chose the upper bunk, Edward climbed into the lower one, and everybody said good night.

Jenny crawled into her basket in the next room, and the Captain went downstairs to smoke his pipe. Outside, the rain beat at the window panes.

"It's good to be indoors on such a night," thought Jenny, with a yawn.

She closed her eyes but could not go to sleep, for she kept worrying about her brothers. It would be terrible if they had run away again.

After a time Jenny crept into her brothers' room. She found that Checkers had come into the lower bunk and cuddled in Edward's arms.

How peacefully the brothers slept! The longer Jenny watched them, the happier she felt. She also felt that someone should be thanked for all this happiness. So she went downstairs and said good night again to Captain Tinker.